GREEK GODS
and *Goddesses*

I AM HADES!

WRITTEN BY
THOMAS KINGSLEY TROUPE

ILLUSTRATED BY
FELISHIA HENDITIRTO

TABLE OF CONTENTS

A Mermaid Book
SEAHORSE PUBLISHING

BOO! Aw, did I scare you?

Well, you should be scared, mortal being! You are in the presence of the Greek god of the underworld. I rule over the place where souls go after death.

Yes, I'm a really scary guy. Let me introduce myself: I am Hades!

Along with my two brothers, I'm one of the three most powerful gods in ancient Greek history. Zeus rules the sky, and Poseidon rules the sea. I ended up reigning over the underworld where things are dark, gloomy, and nasty. But hey, I like it. Let me tell you my story.

I was the first-born son of Cronus, god of time. He ruled over everything from Mount Olympus. He loved being the boss and was afraid of anyone else taking over. So, when my mother Rhea gave birth to my older sisters and me, Cronus swallowed us whole.

I guess Dad thought this would solve his problem. He even swallowed my little brother Poseidon after he was born. We all sat there inside of our father, listening to his stomach rumble, wondering what we were going to do.

A question for you, mortal soul: Have you ever been launched out of someone's stomach? Well, we all were.

It turns out our newest baby brother, Zeus, was hidden by Rhea. When he got older, he gave Cronus some poison. He got sick, and out we came!

Being free from our father's gut was great. No way were we going back in!

So, we fought in a big battle with Daddy Cronus that lasted ten years. He brought out his old-god friends, the Titans, but we kept fighting. Eventually, we won. It was our time to rule!

My brothers and I divided up the world. Was being god of the underworld my first choice? Well, no. But that's how it all worked out.

Zeus was the hero and became king of all the gods, I guess. Poseidon got second choice, and he took the sea. That left the dark place for me.

So, they get to live high on Mount Olympus, and I live in a shadowy palace beneath the earth. It's fine, it's fine.

Really, it's not all bad. I have a great guard dog named Cerberus who has three heads. Trust me, if anyone tried to attack the underworld for some reason, Cerberus would scare the socks right off their feet. He's a real good, er…bad, boy.

Even with Cerberus to keep me company, it gets kind of dark and lonely in the underworld. So, I decided I needed a wife.

I know it seems weird, but I found my sister Demeter's daughter Persephone quite beautiful. And so did everyone else!

A whole bunch of guys liked her, including Ares, Hephaestus, Apollo, and Hermes. But Persephone wasn't interested in being anyone's girlfriend. She told them all to buzz off. Instead, she liked spending her time in nature. You know, with plants and animals.

Persephone's lack of interest wasn't going to stop me. I needed a queen and a wife, and I knew that Persephone was the one.

One day, while she was out in the Nysian meadow with some of her nymph friends, she spotted a beautiful flower. She went to pick it and wandered away from the others. That's when I struck.

I opened up the ground beneath her feet like an earthquake. I rolled up onto the surface in my amazing golden chariot. Before she could move, I kidnapped her. Persephone was mine!

I took Persephone back to the underworld and made her my queen. I was as happy as a dark dude like me can be.

But back up on the surface, my sister Demeter was not happy. She missed her daughter, and she wanted her back.

Demeter was the goddess of agriculture. That means she made crops and plants grow. But since she was busy searching for Persephone, she ignored her duties.

If crops don't grow, big problems happen. Great famines spread across the land, causing untold deaths. Zeus stuck his nose in the matter. He sent Hermes to the underworld to demand that I release Persephone.

But you know what? Zeus isn't the boss of me, even if he is king of the gods.

I had a plan. Before she left with Hermes, I had Persephone eat a few pomegranate seeds. She didn't know that if you eat something in the underworld, part of you is stuck there forever.

Zeus and Demeter still weren't happy, so we made a deal. For eight months of the year, Persephone could live on Mount Olympus. For the other four months, she would live with me in the underworld. The time Persephone was away became winter, when nothing grew. When Persephone returned to the surface, spring flowers bloomed.

Orpheus was a great poet and musician whose music charmed everyone. When his wife Eurydice died, Orpheus was full of grief.

Orpheus knew that, because Eurydice was a mortal, her soul went to the underworld when she died. He could not bear life without her, and he had to find her. So Orpheus decided to make a trek to the underworld.

After a dangerous journey into my realm, Orpheus asked to meet with Persephone and me. He told us how sad Eurydice's death made him. My wife and I took pity on the poor man. We made a deal with him.

Then I Hades, god of the underworld, did something I had never done before for any human. I told Orpheus that he could take his wife back to the land of the living.

However, there was one condition.

Orpheus and Eurydice had to make the long journey out of the underworld without ever looking back. If they succeeded, the two would be reunited in the mortal realm once more.

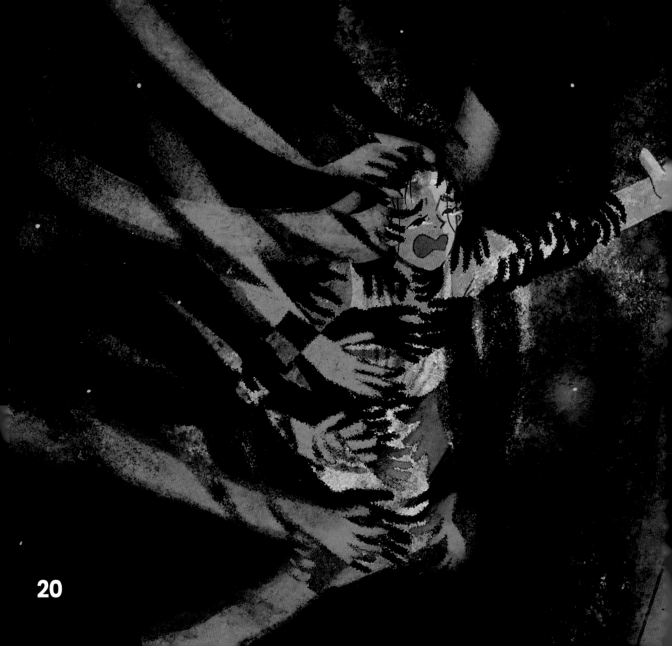

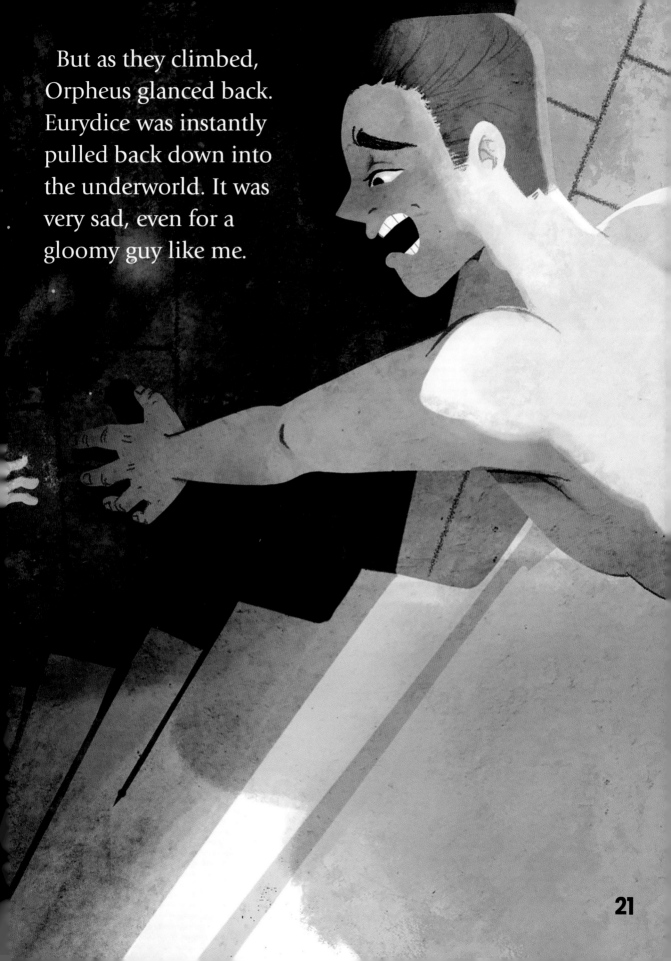

But as they climbed, Orpheus glanced back. Eurydice was instantly pulled back down into the underworld. It was very sad, even for a gloomy guy like me.

And now it is time to say goodbye, mortal reader. As the big, bad, scary god of death, I've likely terrified you enough.

But whenever you hear of death, lost souls, and the darkness of winter, I hope you think of me. Remember, I rule the underworld, kid. I am HADES!

What Is Greek Mythology?

Greek mythology is a collection of epic stories about gods, goddesses, heroes, strange creatures, and the origins of the civilization of ancient Greece. For hundreds of years before they were first written down, the stories were told and retold orally by the ancient Greeks. The tales were passed down over generations and are still known today as myths and legends.

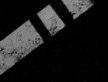

Questions for Discussion

1. Persephone spends part of every year in the underworld. How does this myth help explain real events in nature?

2. How does Hades feel about his life in the underworld? Give evidence from his story to explain your answer.

3. What fact about Hades is your favorite? Explain why.

Writing Activity

Write to describe the underworld. Use your imagination to tell what it looks like, smells like, sounds like, and feels like. What furnishings, decorations, or other items let you know that Hades, Persephone, and Cerberus live there along with the souls of mortals? Draw a picture to illustrate your writing.

About the Author

Thomas Kingsley Troupe is the author of over 200 books for young readers. When he's not writing, he enjoys reading, playing video games, and investigating haunted places with the Twin Cities Paranormal Society. Otherwise, he's probably taking a nap or something. Thomas lives in Woodbury, Minnesota, with his two sons.

About the Illustrator

Felishia Henditirto was born in Bandung, Indonesia, and has been fascinated by art and stories since she was a child. When everybody else in class was busy taking notes, she was stuck in her own world, drawing. She always has a thirst for magic and tries to find it in everything she does, especially in reading! If she is not working, you can find her visiting far, faraway places in the pages of a book.

Written by: Thomas Kingsley Troupe
Illustrated by: Felishia Henditirto
Design by: Under the Oaks Media
Series Development: James Earley
Editor: Kim Thompson

Library of Congress PCN Data
I Am Hades! / Thomas Kingsley Troupe
Greek Gods and Goddesses
ISBN 979-8-8873-5934-2 (hard cover)
ISBN 979-8-8873-5973-1 (paperback)
ISBN 979-8-8904-2032-9 (EPUB)
ISBN 979-8-8904-2091-6 (eBook)
Library of Congress Control Number: 2023912428

Printed in the United States of America.

Seahorse Publishing Company
www.seahorsepub.com

Published in the United States
Seahorse Publishing
PO Box 771325
Coral Springs, FL 33077